Ricky Rat In New Orleans

by

Sharon S. Hurst

Illustrated by

Lyndsie Fugate

AuthorHouse™
1663 Liberty Drive, Suite 200
Bloomington, IN 47403
www.authorhouse.com
Phone: 1-800-839-8640

First published by AuthorHouse 1/22/2008

ISBN: 978-1-4343-6349-7 (sc)

Library of Congress Control Number: 2008900322

Printed in the United States of America
Bloomington, Indiana

This book is printed on acid-free paper.

authorHOUSE®

TO BAILEY, KAILEY AND ALLEN

Ricky Rat is a kind and loving little fuzzy rat with big brown eyes. He smiles at everyone who looks his way. When he flashes his big smile, his eyes twinkle and his big white teeth almost glow. That's because his loving parents have taught him to brush his teeth twice a day. He even flosses his teeth.

They have tried to teach him to be good and kind to everyone. They have taught him to be polite and to keep himself clean. Ricky is their only little Rat and they watch over him all the time so no harm will come to him. Everyone in the rat community loves Ricky.

There are many good rat families living in the city of New Orleans; but of course, as in every city, there are a few young rats who don't do as well in school because they don't study and they don't do their homework as they should. Ricky is always studying very hard in school because he wants to make his family proud of him. He loves to read and he almost always wins his Spelling Bee.

One rat by the name of Robert Rat and is a doctor trained in Rat Foot Surgery. He opens his tiny doctor's office on Cottage Cheese Alley in downtown New Orleans.

Even though Doctor Robert Rat is a foot doctor, he never turns away a sick or injured rat. He is a very kind doctor.

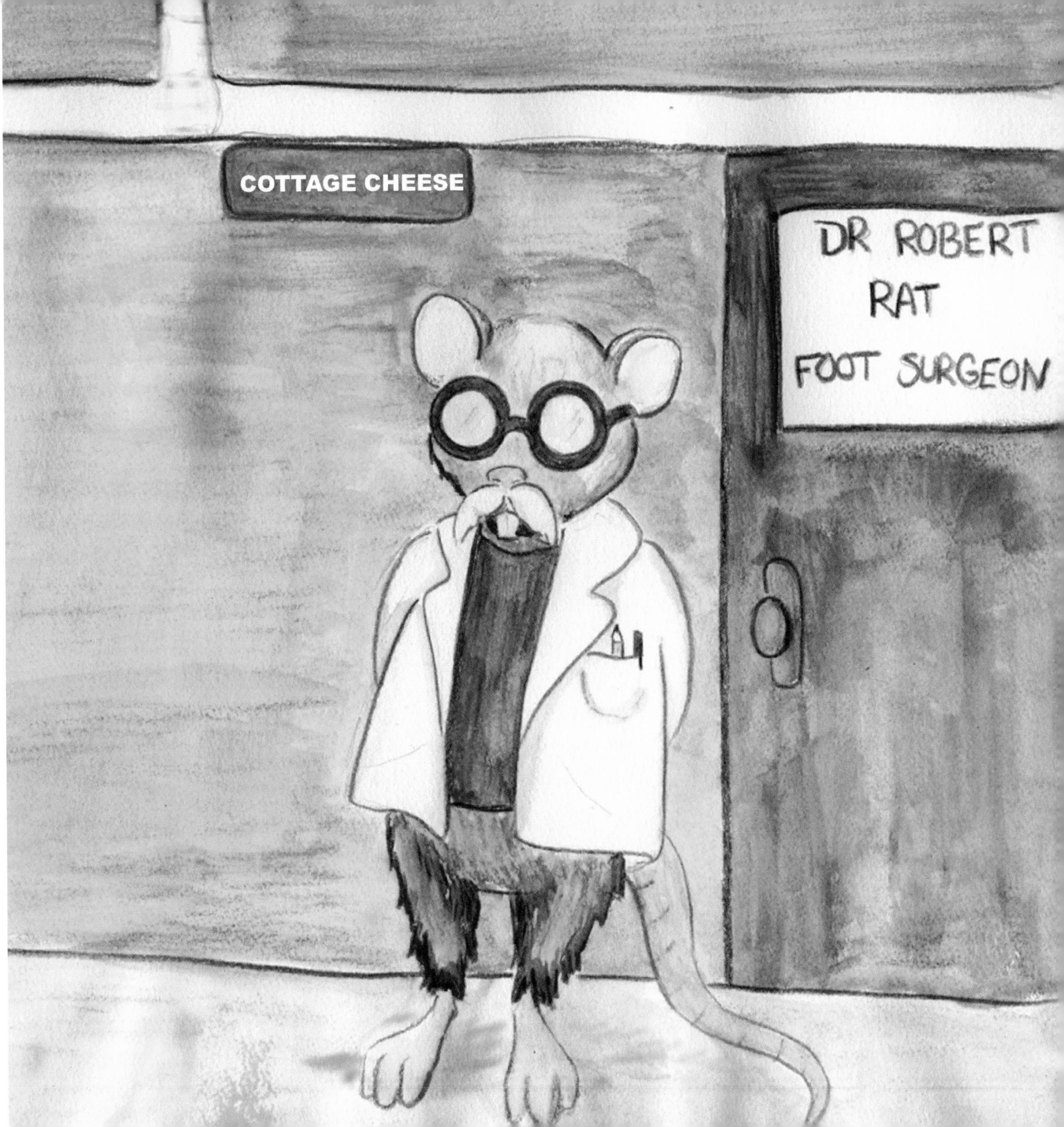
COTTAGE CHEESE
DR ROBERT
RAT
FOOT SURGEON

Dr. Robert Rat hires a lady rat by the name of Miss Rowena Rat. Rowena is tall for a rat. Perhaps that is partly because she likes to wear high heeled shoes with pointed toes. She likes to hear the way they make a clicking noise as she walks around the office. She also wears glasses that are pointed on the outer sides of the bright red frames. Rowena answers the phone and makes the appointments for Doctor Robert Rat's patients.

He also hires a well trained rat to be his nurse. Her name is Nurse Nottingham. She is short and shows the results of eating entirely too many donuts. Her white uniform seems to get tighter every day, but she just keeps eating the donuts she brings with her everyday. Her shoes are big white shoes that have shoestrings in them. She loves to wear long earring, and they sometimes get caught on the collar of her uniform. She wears her nurse's cap with pride and keeps her uniform nice and white all the time. Nurse Nottingham knows her business and is a big help to Doctor Robert Rat.

The streets of New Orleans are always busy, and dangerous, especially during Marti Gras. Marti Gras is a big party that is held out in the streets of downtown New Orleans. People carry food and drinks into the streets and have a party. Of course, much of the food is dropped onto the streets as the people walk through the streets. This is wonderful for all the rats. They don't have to hunt for their food because it is dropped right in front of them.

Ricky Rat is with his parents watching all the crowds of people when he sees part of a hotdog bun fall onto the street. Without thinking, he pulls his little fuzzy hand away from his Momma's hand and runs right into the huge crowd of people. His Momma and Poppa call out to him.

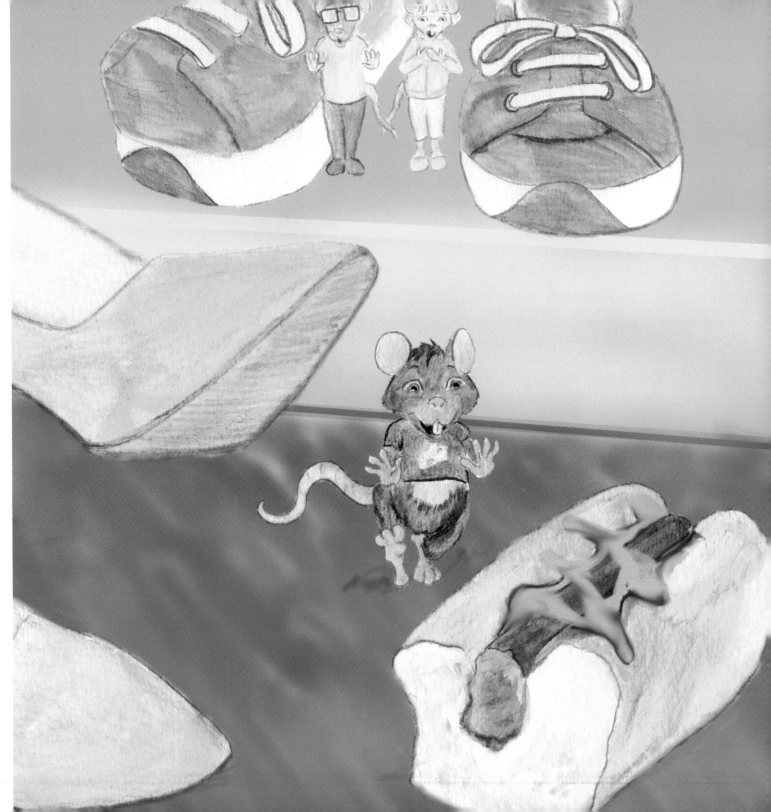

"Ricky, come back. You'll be hurt!"

It's too late! Someone, a human, has stepped on his back leg!

He yells and calls for his Momma.

"Momma, help me! I can't walk! I can't run! Please help me!"

His Poppa and Momma look to the right and they look to their left. Then they both run right into the crowd hoping they can reach their beloved Ricky before someone else comes along and steps directly on him and maybe even kills him. They are both sick with worry. Can they reach him in time? Will he be unhurt other than his injured leg? Only time will tell!

Ricky's Poppa grabs him under his arms and his Momma grabs his legs, being careful to place his long tail over his stomach. They run as fast as they can to dodge all the people's huge feet. They run this way and that way until they are safely in an old alley. They carefully lay their precious little Ricky on an old oily, soft rag that has been tossed into the alley.

By this time several other worried rats have gathered to see what has happened.

"I have my cell phone in the pocket of my leather jacket. I'll call the Rat Ambulance!" Rosco Rat calls out.

Momma Rat, who by now, is kneeling down beside Ricky. She looks up through sobbing eyes and begs Rosco Rat, "Hurry and place the call for an ambulance."

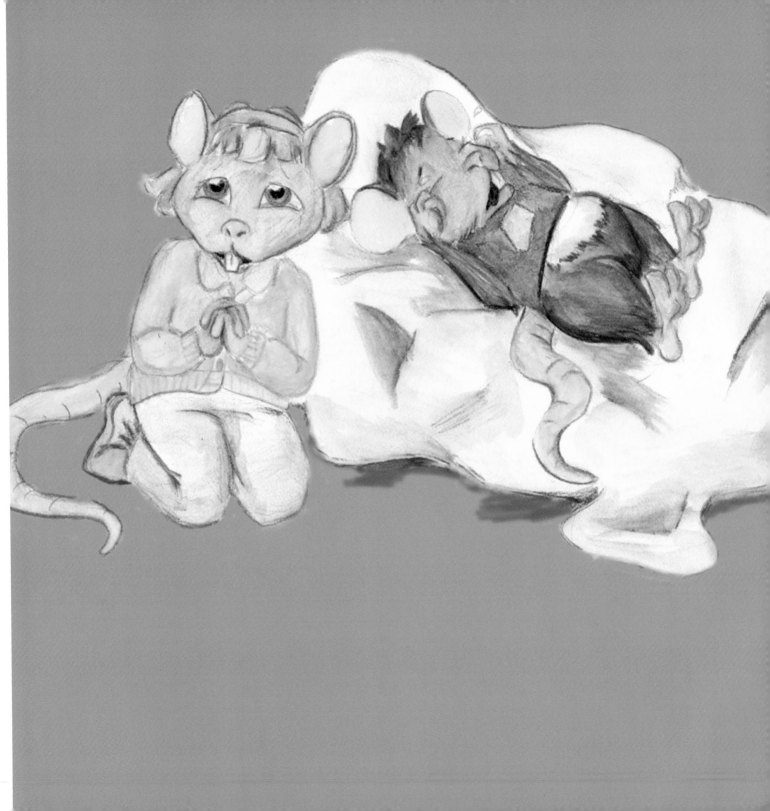

Rosco Rat reaches for his cell phone and tries to dial the number, but his cell phone battery is dead. He cannot place the call. "Oh, no!" Momma Rat exclaims. "Now what will we do?"

Rosco Rat begins shouting to all the other rats to try to locate a cell phone that will work. Success! In a matter of seconds, but what seems like hours to Ricky's Momma, a second cell phone is located and the call is placed to the Rat Ambulance Company of New Orleans. In just a few moments they can all hear the welcome sound of the siren scurrying in and around the feet of all the people in the street. An adult rat volunteers to be brave and he runs out into the street to direct the Rat Ambulance to the correct alley. The rats all fear the ambulance will not be able to locate the injured Ricky in time.

The driver of the ambulance and his assistant are both adult rats dressed in little white coats. Once they arrive in the alley, they jump out, run to the back of the ambulance, open the back door and lift out the cot. They scurry to the little injured rat stretched out on the soft, oily rag. Ricky is sobbing softly. Big tears are rolling down his fuzzy cheeks. His leg really hurts. They quickly, but carefully, place him in the back of the ambulance.

His Momma and Poppa both climb inside the ambulance and sit on each side of him. They each hold one of his fuzzy little hands. They try to be brave for their little son. They tell him he will be fine just as soon as they can get him to Dr. Robert Rat's office.

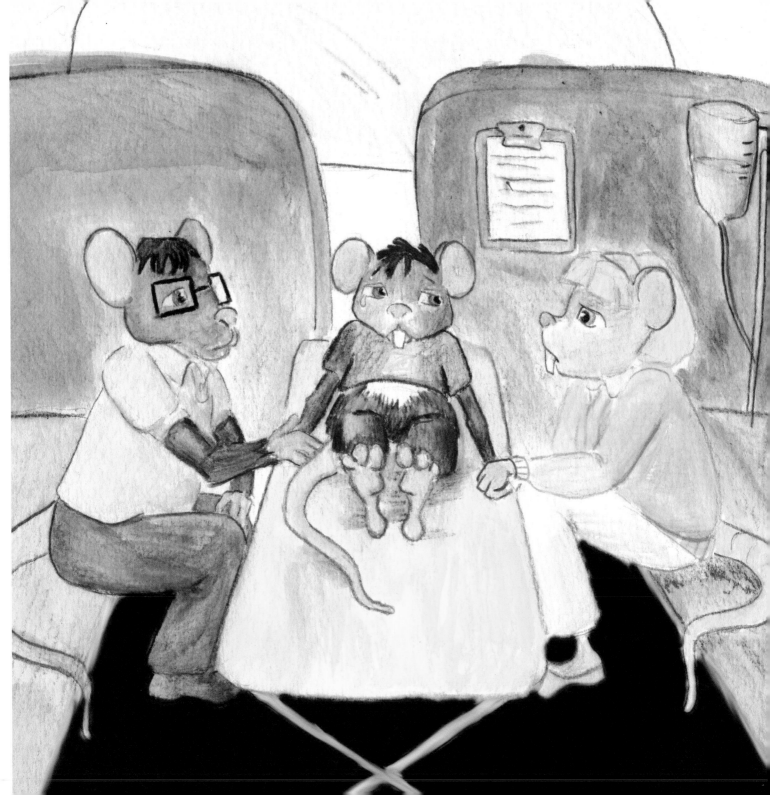

They can all hear the siren squealing as the ambulance dodges the hundreds and hundreds of huge feet in the streets. The ambulance is constantly hitting big bumps in the street. The bumps are pieces of hotdogs and trash that have been thrown on the street by the people.

Finally, they screech into Dr. Robert's driveway. The two ambulance rats, with their white coats flowing out behind them, jump out of their ambulance and run to the back. They quickly open the back door and remove the cot holding little Ricky. They rush to the front door of Dr. Robert Rat's office, open the door and carry in Ricky.

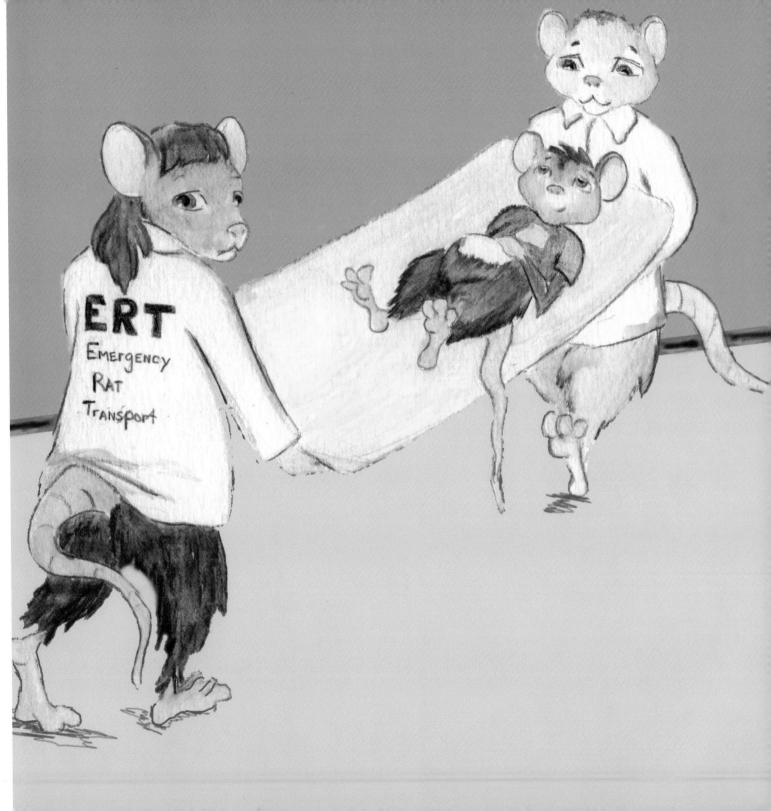

Nurse Nottingham Rat has heard all the noise and comes running in. She sees there is an emergency and shouts for Dr. Robert Rat to come at once. He comes into the room immediately.

"Well, well, what do we have here?" Doctor Robert Rat asks calmly. "Let's bring this little fella back into my examining room so I can get a better look at him. Come on, Momma and Poppa. You can come back with him, also."

WAITING
ROOM

He calmly sits Momma and Poppa Rat down and he begins to examine Ricky's leg.

"Hmmmmmm, it looks like this little guy has a broken leg."

"Oh, no!" Momma Rat says.

"Now, now, Momma Rat, this is nothing serious. Why don't you and Poppa Rat go out front with my nice office helper, Miss Rowena, while Nurse Nottingham and I fix up this little guy?"

Little Ricky is scared but he has heard how kind Dr. Robert Rat is and his leg REALLY does hurt! Dr. Robert Rat tells Ricky to hold Nurse Nottingham's hand while he sets his broken leg. Next, he asks Ricky what color cast he wants.

"You mean I can have whatever color I want?"

"That's what I said!"

"I WANT PURPLE!!!" Ricky shouts.

"Then purple it shall be."

Dr. Robert Rat asks Ricky's Momma and Poppa to come back and see their little Ricky.

"LOOK! I have a purple cast on my leg! I'll be the only rat in New Orleans with a purple cast on my leg! Isn't it great?"

Dr. Robert Rat loans Ricky a pair of crutches so Ricky can get back home. He is smiling and is so proud of his purple cast. His Momma and Poppa are smiling, too. They aren't smiling because of the purple cast, but because they know how lucky their little Ricky is to be alive and well. So Momma and Poppa Rat and little Ricky Rat go to their cozy home.

Momma and Poppa Rat gently put their beloved Ricky to bed and tuck him in. They pull his favorite blue quilt up under his little chin. His Momma made it for him for his last birthday. He loves his blue quilt because it always makes him feel safe.

They are very careful not to hurt his little broken leg. They both kiss little Ricky on his little fuzzy cheeks and tell him how much they love him. He looks up into their eyes with tears in his eyes. "I love you both so much, Momma and Poppa. You saved my life tonight."

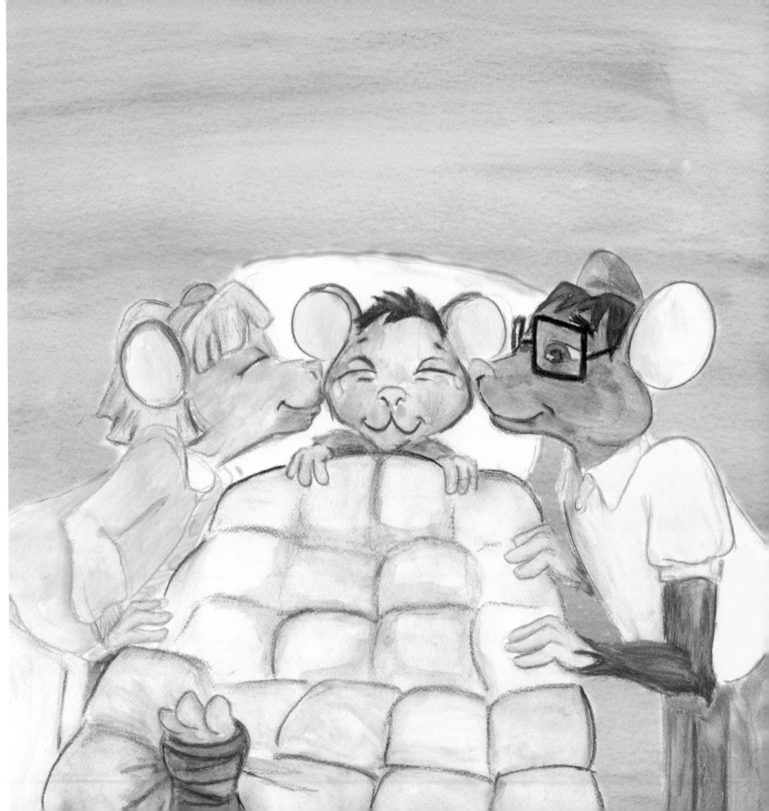

They turn on the little night light for Ricky so he will feel safe.
Ricky looks over to see his Momma and Poppa as they walk
out of his room holding hands. He smiles because he knows his
parents love each other so much and he also knows they love him.
Momma and Poppa are both so grateful that their little Ricky is
safely tucked into his bed.
This little Rat family has much for which to be thankful. Their
family is safe and they are together in their warm, cozy home.

THE END